MW00912004

Nerfnerd

By Melanie Michael

Illustrated by John Alderton

Frankie and Cori,
May you find your most wonderful life!
Melanie ♥

Headline Kids
an imprint of **Headline Books, Inc.**
Terra Alta, WV

Nerfnerd

by Melanie Michael
illustrated by John Alderton

Headline Kids
P. O. Box 52
Terra Alta, WV 26764
www.headlinekids.com
Tel: 800-570-5951
Email: mybook@headlinebooks.com

www.headlinebooks.com
www.headlinekids.com

Published by Headline Books

Headline Kids is an imprint of Headline Books

ISBN-13: 978-0-938467-07-6

Library of Congress Cataloging-in-Publication Data

Michael, Melanie.
 Nerfnerd / Melanie Michael ; illustrated by John Alderton.
    p. cm.
 Summary: After being rediscovered by a little girl, a sock puppet has a chance to become a beloved toy once again.
 ISBN 978-0-938467-07-6
 [1. Puppets--Fiction. 2. Toys--Fiction. 3. Socks--Fiction.] I. Alderton, John, ill. II. Title.
 PZ7.M57981Ne 2011
 [Fic]--dc22
                            2011000056

PRINTED IN THE UNITED STATES OF AMERICA

Nerfnerd lay at the very bottom of his shoebox feeling sorry for himself again. It was all he had been able to manage these past few days. Because our friend Nerfnerd had the unfortunate luck of being a sock puppet. If you think no one listens to you now because you are a child, try being a sock puppet. And not just any sock puppet, but an insignificant, gray-mouse sock puppet.

Not quite toy enough for the toy box, and not entirely sock, Nerfnerd had to share a shoebox in the back of the closet with two friends: a baby doll head from three Christmases ago (the kind of head that keeps popping off its own body) and a dried out dill pickle spear that had been on the dinner plate of a famous 1980's movie star.

Life for Nerfnerd was, from what he could tell, decidedly pitiful. That was until one day when mother made the little girl who owned Nerfnerd clean out her closet.

On that life-changing day, as Nerfnerd lay slumped over in his shoebox, the little girl dug into a heap of dirty clothes and other "closety" type items until Nerfnerd's protective shoebox came tumbling out from under the heap in the back of the closet. Suddenly the lid popped off and Nerfnerd could see light through his button eyes. Before he could blink, the little girl swept him up just as a bottle of sand art crashed, pouring into the shoebox in a rainbow avalanche. It coated the pickle and blanketed the baby doll's head like a multi-colored wig.

"Look, Mommy! I found Nerfnerd!" the little girl said, hugging the sock puppet's squashy body.

"Emily, what have you been eating?" Mother said in disgust. She snatched Nerfnerd from the little girl and gave him a sniff, "Why, it's ketchup!" she said as she ever so slightly stuck the tippity-tip of her tongue to Nerfnerd.

Yes, Nerfnerd had a rather large ketchup stain that covered his whole nose, most of one button-eye, and about half of his right ear. He remembered the day, not too long ago, when he and the little girl had shared a ketchup-loaded hot dog together (Nerfnerd receiving the bulk of the ketchup in that circumstance).

Mother flung Nerfnerd. He went somersaulting through the air, spiraled into a wall, slid in an upside down fashion, landed, bouncing once, and skidded on the hardwood floor next to the little girl.

"Put it in the hamper, Emily!" Mother said wiping her hands together. "Who knows when that THING was last washed and how many people have had their hands on it!"

Emily picked Nerfnerd up, dangerously dangling him over the garbage can, but tossed him into the dirty clothes hamper instead.

"Lucky to be here," Nerfnerd thought to himself.

He just lay there. It was pretty much all he had done for most of his life except for the rare occasion when the little girl would put him on and make him talk in those awful, squeaky voices.

You see, the bad thing about being a sock puppet is that people make you say the strangest things in the oddest voices; Things that you would never say in real life and you have to just deal with it.

"Don't worry, be happy!" you might say with an incredibly bad and fake Jamaican accent. Or you could be made to croak like a frog when you are clearly NOT a frog and very much a mouse-type sock puppet. And you might be made to sing at the tippity-top of your lungs, "Peanut Butter and Jelly, I have none, but toast and butter, gimme some!"

And there's really nothing that can be done about it at all—because, well...you're a sock puppet.

He had to admit, the girl was all right. The absolute worst thing she would make him do was wear a tiny flowered hat on his little, pointy head and have him play Tea Party with her and talk in dreadfully high voices.

But the little girl's brother? That was an entirely DIFFERENT matter! The little girl's brother would poke poor Nerfnerd with action figures, ramming them into his soft, cushy sock-puppet body. Once, the boy turned Nerfnerd inside out (how very perplexed and out of sorts one feels to be turned inside out) but that wasn't the HALF of it!

The boy turned him inside out, stretching poor Nerfnerd this way and that with both rotten-boy hands, and wore him on his foot—of all places! Can you imagine the humiliation Nerfnerd felt? If he had been a bit more significant he would have been insulted, but he was a sock puppet, so what did it matter?

Nerfnerd noticed a pair of brown socks and then a large, gray sock tumble into the hamper with him. He got an idea. Maybe his mother was HERE in this hamper, waiting for him, to bring him home to the sock drawer with her. He began to look around nervously.

"Mother? Mother, are you here?" he shouted.

All the other articles of clothing turned away from Nerfnerd, except for one little handkerchief; "Mommy! Is that a...? Why it is, Mommy! It's a sock puppet!"

The other articles of clothing kept silent as the little handkerchief spoke.

"Look away, dear," The older, bigger handkerchief warned, "That sock puppet doesn't want to talk to you."

"Oh, but I do!" said Nerfnerd.

Just then the hamper swayed back and forth several times, rocking and tilting. It felt and sounded as if they were being transported up or down a flight of stairs: Nerfnerd couldn't tell.

At once the clothes began sliding and rolling out of the hamper. Some of the younger clothes were yelling, "Whee!"

Others, mainly the older, more set in their way clothes protested, "Not again, not again! Fight the injustice!"

Nerfnerd found himself in water, swishing round and round in a swirl of wet material. Most of the clothes struggled and then, defeated, submitted to the tidal wave forces of the clothes washer. Somehow Nerfnerd managed to stay afloat in the sea of textiles.

"Hi!" he heard someone say.

Nerfnerd found himself swimming right next to a little ball with tiny slits all over its top and bottom.

"My name's Softy," the ball said.

"I'm Nerfnerd. Glad to meet you."

"Y-you don't belong here? Do you?" Softy said.

"Why do you ask?"

"You just don't look like a sock. Uh, I mean, you're too... fancy."

"Well you're not a piece of clothing and YOU'RE here, aren't you?"

"That's different. I BELONG in the washer. I have a very important job in this place. I'm a fabric softener ball," Softy said, "I make sure all the clothes come out of the wash being their softest and smelling their freshest. I just wish..." Softy's voice trailed off.

"What do you wish, Softy?" Nerfnerd asked.

The washer gently shook the two.

Softy looked overwhelmed. "I sit alone in the dark, sometimes for hours, sometimes for days, until another load of clothing comes along. It's awfully lonesome and incredibly boring to just sit by one's self all the time."

Nerfnerd thought about his box, with the baby-doll-head and pickle-spear friends. It had been dark in the box, but never lonely.

"I wish...I wish I didn't belong here," Softy said, "On top of everything else, I have motion sickness. Each day I'm filled up with this goopy liquid and I get...Whoa!"

Suddenly the washer went on full-speed-ahead-spin-cycle. The clothes spun faster and faster. "See what I mean?" Softy cried, "Just when I'm pulled from the washer and filled with goop and I think this time I might get away --- PLOP! Back into the washer I go. I wish I were a sock puppet like you. It must be so fun..."

A hand reached in and started taking all of the clothes out. Nerfnerd felt the hand reach around his soft, wet body.

"Goodbye, Softy!"

"Goodbye, Nerfnerd!"

Nerfnerd looked back once more at Softy. He was the only thing left in the washer. Then the lid slammed shut on poor Softy.

Mother hung all the clothes out to dry on a clothesline, "So they'll smell fresh like last time and we'll save energy, too," she reminded the little girl and her chubby brother, who were helping.

The chubby boy picked up Nerfnerd and rammed a clothespin down over one of Nerfnerd's ears. It pinched him to hang by only an ear.

After a small amount of time went by, Mother gathered all the clothes in a pile, folding the laundry.

When she was done, she set Nerfnerd on top of a pile of multicolored t-shirts.

In a little while, the boy (of all people) came along and snatched Nerfnerd up. His filthy, rotten-boy hands pushed Nerfnerd into the bottom of his gym bag. The bag reeked of bologna and sweat. As he waited out the terribly stinky night, Nerfnerd wondered how long he would have to endure this treatment.

At recess the next day, the boy pulled Nerfnerd from his smelly confines.

"Oh, No!" Nerfnerd thought, "What will happen next?"

The boy had him. The boy scooped him up with his fat fingers and stretched him over his rotten, chubby hand.

"Hey, Billy!" The boy said menacingly.

Little Billy, a poor, hapless child came toddling over.

"Turn around!" the boy demanded.

Like clockwork Billy turned.

Using Nerfnerd's mouth, the boy reached down the backside of Billy's pants and scooped up a handful of Billy's underwear in one powerful swoop.

"Ow!" cried Billy.

"Ow!" Cried...his underwear?

Yes, Nerfnerd was sure he'd heard it.

"What?" Nerfnerd mumbled with a mouthful of undergarment.

The boy yanked harder using Nerfnerd's mouth as a barrier between himself and Billy's unhappy underwear.

"How miserable this is for me!" Nerfnerd sighed.

"Ow!" the underwear cried again, "You could always be me!" It shouted.

Its seams ripped and tore as Billy rose off the ground. Nerfnerd reluctantly tugged at Billy and his undergarment.

"Mercy, Mercy!" Billy and his underwear screamed.

The boy let go of Billy and he toppled to the ground, rubbing his backside and tucking his underwear in.

When the boy and Nerfnerd were home again, the little girl confronted her brother.

"Have you seen Nerfnerd?" She asked, "Mother says she folded him and put him on top of YOUR t-shirt pile."

The boy turned, red-handed, with gym bag behind his back now.

"No, I haven't seen Nerfnerd," he lied.

As he fibbed, he managed to open a cabinet drawer and shove Nerfnerd in.

Tears were forming in the little girls eyes, "If you see him, can you give him to me?" she sniffled, "I want to play Tea Party and it's no fun without him."

"Sure," the boy lied again, and slid the drawer shut on poor Nerfnerd.

"Ahoy Matey! Who be ye?" Nerfnerd heard a voice say from somewhere in the drawer.

He looked around as his button-eyes adjusted to the dark.

In the dim light he could make out a picture postcard with what appeared to be a pirate on it. On the front of the postcard, the pirate smiled a wide, menacing grin. The writing underneath said, "Wish you could be here with me...but I know what a lily libbered land lubber you are!"

As his eyes continued to adjust, Nerfnerd saw that someone had taken the liberty to pencil in a few of the pirate's teeth, scratch an oversized wart onto his big piratey-nose, and give him what seemed to be a very fake mustache.

"Is that you, Mr. Pirate?" Nerfnerd said cautiously.

"Arrr!" said the pirate.

"I'll take that as a yes." Nerfnerd chuckled timidly.

"Are ye a pirate, too?" the pirate asked.

"No, Mr. Pirate. I'm a sock puppet."

"A sock what?"

"Puppet," Nerfnerd said sheepishly.

"A puppet, Poppet?" The pirate said disapprovingly, "Well, shiver me timbers and call me yellow-bellied!

25

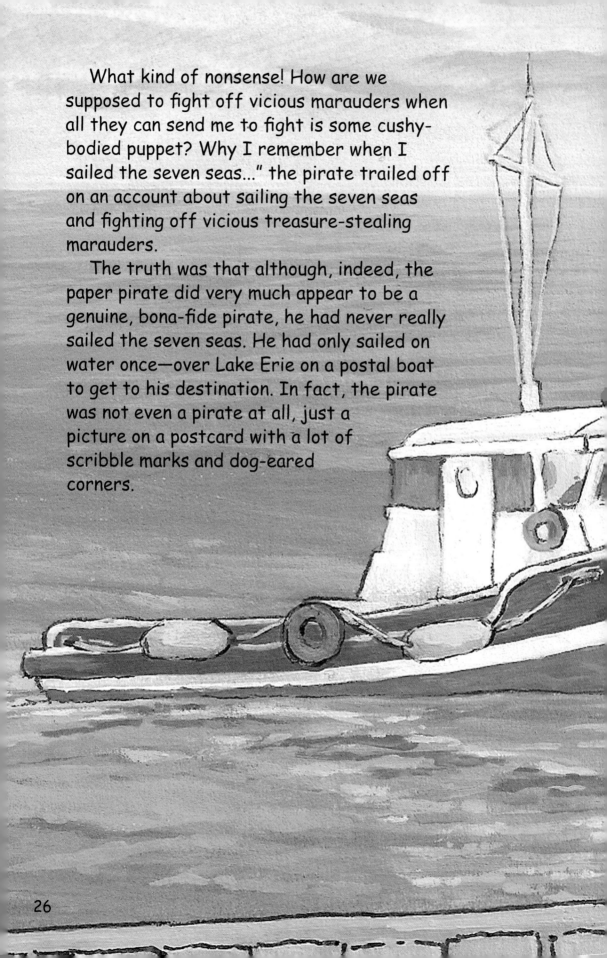

What kind of nonsense! How are we supposed to fight off vicious marauders when all they can send me to fight is some cushy-bodied puppet? Why I remember when I sailed the seven seas..." the pirate trailed off on an account about sailing the seven seas and fighting off vicious treasure-stealing marauders.

The truth was that although, indeed, the paper pirate did very much appear to be a genuine, bona-fide pirate, he had never really sailed the seven seas. He had only sailed on water once—over Lake Erie on a postal boat to get to his destination. In fact, the pirate was not even a pirate at all, just a picture on a postcard with a lot of scribble marks and dog-eared corners.

Nerfnerd could see through this right away and he wondered how many years this postcard pirate had laid in the drawer thinking about sailing the seas and doing piratey things. Nerfnerd shook his head, What a sad, boring life! he thought, To pretend you are something you're not and wait for a day that may never come.

"No offense, Mr. Pirate, but you ARE only made of paper," Nerfnerd said, bravely.

This made the pirate angry, "Mutiny! Mutiny! You'll walk the plank for this!" he bellowed.

Just then the drawer opened and fingers fumbled around for...

"Ah, Nerfnerd!"

It was the little girl again. She slipped him on over her petite, little-girl hand and wore him up to her room. She gathered the tea party fare: a frilly-lace tablecloth, a stout teapot, fancy cups and saucers with dainty, blue roses, a clear-glass vase with dusty, fake flowers, and adorable pink pillows for all the dolls to sit on. A beautiful china doll with curly, black hair sat across the table from Nerfnerd. He blushed a little at the sight of the doll.

"I'll be right back, Nerfnerd. I need to ask Mother to make the tea for us to drink. Don't leave!" the little girl said with a giggle, looking back at his limp body slumped on the table.

When she was gone he looked around.

The cups and saucers rocked back and forth on their bottoms. The china doll smiled at Nerfnerd and Nerfnerd blushed again.

One of the saucers looked around the room suspiciously and then complained to poor Nerfnerd, "We never get to leave this table, only to be washed and rinsed and then set back on the table again."

"You think you have it bad? I can't even leave this chair," the china doll said softly. "Look, I'm tied to the back so that the little girl won't pick me up and break me." The china doll pointed to a pink satin rope tying her to the chair. Her perfect, pouting lips bowed down into a frown, "You're lucky! You get to move about freely with the little girl."

"Yes!" all the tired, dusty flowers in the vase shouted.

"And she parades you around on her hand. How very exciting that must be and how very important you must look!" the teapot spouted.

In that moment, Nerfnerd, our friend, thought about how his life compared to the lives of those he'd met on his journey. He realized that living life as a sock puppet really wasn't so bad:

He wasn't stuck in one place or forced to do a lonely job that made his tummy twirl, like Softy.

He wasn't a pair of underwear on little Billy, going places but never really seeing anything or being stretched beyond his limits.

He didn't sit in a drawer day after day pretending to be something he wasn't, waiting for a day that may never come, like the mean, old postcard pirate.

And he wasn't tied down to a chair to keep from getting broken like the beautiful china doll.

His life was, well...different.

Sometimes it was dark in his shoe box, but he always had his friends, the doll head and the pickle spear, to keep him company. Sometimes he was made to do some pretty silly things like talk in squeaky, high voices and attend tea parties in a ridiculous hat, but he was loved by the little girl. And even in his worst times with the chubby, rotten boy, Nerfnerd was flexible enough to take it; with his soft, cushy body, he didn't have to worry about getting broken.

He may never find his mother. Maybe he never even HAD a mother to take him home to the sock drawer. He might never get the chance to live in the toy box with real, genuine toys, but that was okay, too. Nerfnerd decided his life as a sock puppet was, on the whole...good. For the first time, Nerfnerd was happy to be who he was—an insignificant, gray-mouse sock puppet.

Just then, the little girl returned with a tray of sugar cookies and lemon flavored tea. She slipped Nerfnerd over her tiny hand and placed the flowered hat on his pointy head.

"Would you like some tea?" Nerfnerd said to the china doll in that familiar, dreadfully high voice...and he smiled.